*In memory of Andrew Hollingsworth
– a very special children's bookseller.*

First published in Great Britain in 1993 by Andersen Press Ltd., 20 Vauxhall Bridge Road, London SW1V 2SA. Published in Australia by Random House Australia Pty., 20 Alfred Street, Milsons Point, Sydney, NSW 2061. All rights reserved. Colour separated in Switzerland by Photolitho AG, Offsetreproduktionen, Gossau, Zurich. Printed and bound in Italy by Grafiche AZ, Verona.

10 9 8 7 6 5 4 3 2 1

British Library Cataloguing in Publication Data available.
ISBN 0 86264 373 2

This book has been printed on acid-free paper

THE
SCHOOLBUS COMES
AT EIGHT O'CLOCK

Written and Illustrated by

David McKee

Andersen Press · London

"Why don't we have any clocks?" said Eric.
"Yes, everyone has at least one," said Jennifer.
"We don't need a clock," said Mr Giles.
"Time isn't *so* important. Anyway here
comes the school bus so we know it's eight
o'clock. Bye-bye."
"A clock would look rather nice, dear,"
said Mrs Giles as the children left.

On Saturday morning they went to the market. Among the antiques they saw a grandfather clock.

"It would look lovely beside the front door," said Mrs Giles. They bought the clock.

"We'll start it as soon as we get home," said Eric, excitedly.

"We can't," laughed Mrs Giles. "We don't know what time it is. We'll have to wait until Monday morning, when the school bus comes at eight o'clock."

On Monday morning Mr Giles started the clock. When the children returned from school they rushed to look at the time.
"Four o'clock," said Jennifer. The clock struck four.
"Dad thinks it's too loud," said Mrs Giles. "We'll get used to it."
"Teatime is at five o'clock," said Eric.
"Oh really," said Mrs Giles. "Then bedtime is at eight o'clock."
"Oh!" said the children.

That night no-one slept well, as the clock struck every hour.
"We'll get used to it," said Mrs Giles.
In the morning the children got ready and watched the clock.
It struck eight.
"Eight o'clock," said Jennifer. "The school bus comes at eight o'clock. Goodbye."
A little while later the children came back in again.
"The bus hasn't come," said Eric. "The clock must be wrong."

When the clock showed half past eight the school bus
arrived.
"Sorry we're late," said the driver. "We had a
puncture."
"There, the clock wasn't wrong," said Mrs Giles.
"It could have been," said Jennifer, "we would never
have known."
"She's right," said Mr Giles as he waved goodbye.

Later that day Mr Giles returned with another clock.
"Now we'll know if the clock's wrong," he said.
At first all went well, but gradually there was a slight
difference in the clocks. At midnight there were twenty
four chimes. Everyone was awake.
"We'll get used to it," said Mrs Giles.
"We'll get used to it," said Jennifer.

The next morning the children argued about
which clock was wrong. When the school bus
came they weren't ready. The bus had to wait.

Later, Mr Giles came home with another clock.
"With three clocks we'll know which is wrong," he
said.
"Four," laughed Mrs Giles. "A salesman came by
and I bought a cuckoo clock."
They spent so much time with the clocks that Mrs
Giles had to hurry to get tea ready in time.

When the children came home they were pleased. "Now we really will know what time it is," said Jennifer.
Mr Giles wasn't so sure. The clocks weren't striking quite together and the cuckoos came after the others.

When Mrs Giles called the children for bed they complained.

"Not yet, I'm winning," said Eric.

"Net yet, I want to catch him up," said Jennifer.

"It's eight o'clock," said Mrs Giles. "Bedtime."

"I didn't hear the cuckoos," said Eric.

"It's slow," said Mrs Giles.

At midnight the whole family was awake again.
There were thirty six chimes followed by twelve
cuckoos.

"Dad," said Eric. "How long does
it take to get used to it?"
"Too long," said his father.

The next morning the house was quiet. There was only one clock, the grandfather one. Even that was silent. The hands pointed at eight o'clock.

"Where are the clocks?" asked Eric.

"I've got rid of them," said Mr Giles. "This one stays because your mother likes it there, but it stays stopped," he added. "You know a fast clock is never right, and a slow clock is never right, but a stopped clock is right twice a day."

"Yes," said Eric. "When the school bus comes."

Jennifer laughed. "And at bedtime."

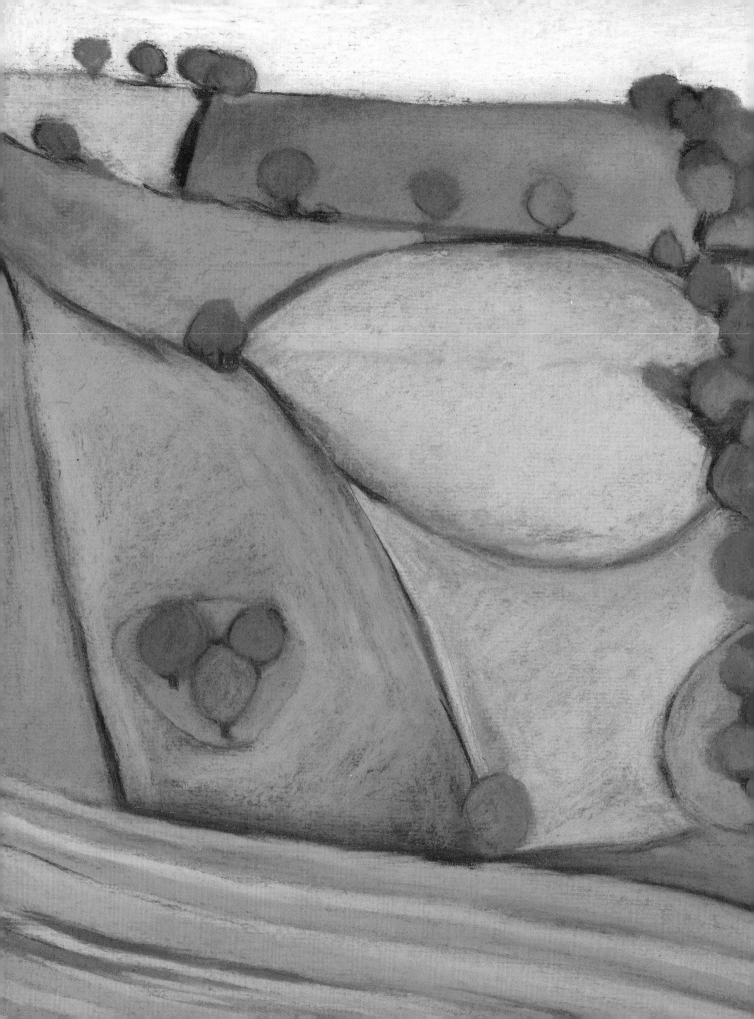